Words change worlds

• • •

For my three little inspirations: Grace, Luke, & Lily.
Love makes everything grow.
B. C.

For my boys, Sutter, Graham, & Sean.
You make me bloom.
S. S. S.

For my boys, Charlie and Jimmy.
I love you to the moon and back!
G. S.

• • •

This book was typeset in Chaparral.
The illustrations were created digitally.

Published 2017 by
Two Hoots Press
Asheville, NC
www.twohootspress.com

Cate's Magic Garden

Betsy Coffeen and Samantha Steiger Smith

illustrated by Ginger Seehafer

Two Hoots Press

Davey Dung Beetle,
Walter Worm,
and Pete Potato Bug
trudged through their garden —
and boy were they mad.

"Our plants are shriveled! We have no food, and there isn't any shade for a home," they grumbled.

"We're hot, hungry, dried up, and fed up! What'll we do?"

"Maybe I can help,"
a small voice said.

The grumpy group of friends looked up
to find a caterpillar smiling at them.

"How can *you* help?" asked Davey.
"You're just a tiny caterpillar."

"Oh, I know a little something about change," Cate said.

"Besides, I come from a garden that's filled with leaves as large as elephant ears and colorful petals as plump as pillows."

"But why listen to me?
I'm just a tiny caterpillar."

Cate turned to inch away.

"Wait!" said Davey, moving closer.
"We'll do anything to make our garden
grow. We've tried watering and weeding,
but nothing is working."

"Living things need much more than that.
They also need to know you love them.
So you have to tell them, of course."

"Tell them?" huffed Davey.
"Plants don't talk. And they definitely
don't listen!" he added, poking
at a dead stem.

"Maybe there's a better way
to encourage them," said Cate.

She wrapped herself around a wilted leaf
and whispered softly . . . .

The sad little leaf shuddered
and then, like magic,
stood a bit prouder.

"Wow!" Walter said.
"How on earth did
you do that?"

"Let me try!" said Davey.

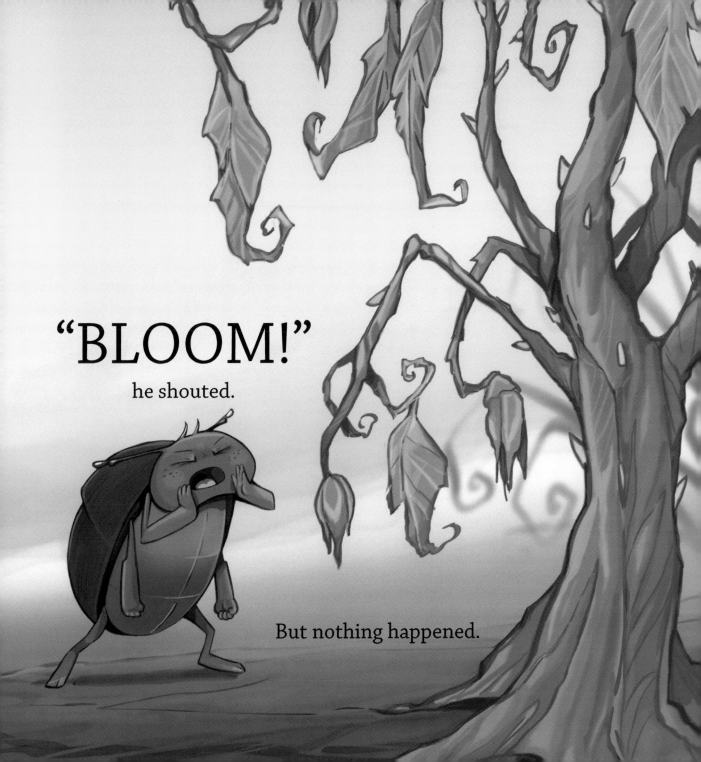

"Bloom right now!"
Davey demanded.

But the rose bush only bent
to the ground.

"It's hopeless," sighed Pete.
"Words won't change anything."

"Try again," Cate said. She was
a very patient caterpillar.
"Words can change worlds."

"How?" asked Pete.

"Well," Cate said. "It depends on which words you choose — and how you say them. Words can lift you up, but they can also drag you down."

Davey took a deep breath. "Please grow little rose bush," he said in a small voice. "I *know* you can do it . . . if you try."

Then something amazing happened.
The rose bush stretched up as bright blossoms burst from its stems.

"I can't believe it!" Pete exclaimed.

"It worked!" Walter laughed.

"See?" Cate said. "There's hope for this garden, yet. But it will take every kind word you know to make it grow."

Davey, Pete, and Walter went right to work.

Davey chatted with
the daisies.

Pete talked with
the petunias.

Walter showered the garden with love
(and plenty of water).

And then one day . . .

Davey stared in wonder
at the beautiful garden.

"Thank you, Cate!"
he called out.

But Cate was nowhere in sight.
Davey, Pete, and Walter had been
so busy gardening, they hadn't
noticed that Cate was gone.

The friends searched high and low.

"Where is she?" cried Pete.
"Cate brought our garden back to
life. We have to thank her!"

"Look," Walter whispered. "She's in there."

"Whoa!" said Pete.

"Wow!" said Davey. They moved closer to the chrysalis.

The three friends knew just what to do.

"You can do it!" said Davey.

"We believe in you!" said Pete.

"We'll be right here when
you're ready!" said Walter.

And they were.

Betsy Coffeen is a mom, a Childhelp Wings Advisor, and freelance writer, trying to make the world a better place one word at a time. She lives in Paradise Valley, Arizona with her husband Clay and three children. She enjoys running, yoga, traveling with her family, and devoting her time to serving the children of Childhelp. She especially wants to thank her husband, Minnesota family, cherished cousin Stephanie, and dear friend Jamie Relei Ferguson.

Samantha Steiger Smith is a freelance writer and author who lives with her husband and two sons in Pittsburgh, PA. She spearheads the kids Summer Brain Food program with the Food Bank, and loves supporting Childhelp. She wishes to thank her family, Team CATE, and her editor, Amy Cherrix, for bringing Cate to life.

Ginger Seehafer is a commercial illustrator residing and working in the Chicago suburbs. She loves working from her home, surrounded by her family, friends, and cats. Ginger also illustrated the picture book, *Rudy's New Human*, and enjoys volunteering to teach local students how to create art themselves.

CPSIA information can be obtained
at www.ICGtesting.com
Printed in the USA
LVIC04n1916291017
553850LV00002BA/3